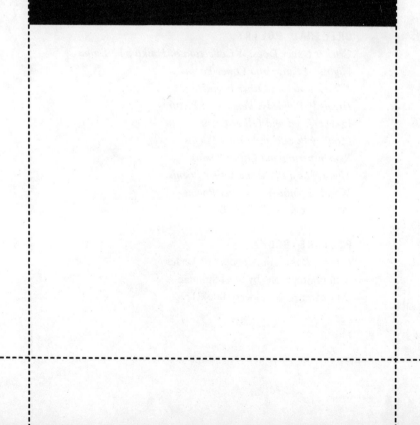

# I Am Writing a Poem About...

## A Game of Poetry

## Other books by Myra Cohn Livingston:

**ANTHOLOGIES**

*A Time to Talk: Poems of Friendship*
*Call Down the Moon: Poems of Music*
*Dilly Dilly Piccalilli: Poems for the Very Young*
*If the Owl Calls Again: A Collection of Owl Poems*
*I Like You, If You Like Me: Poems of Friendship*
*Lots of Limericks*
*Poems of Christmas*
*Riddle-Me Rhymes*
*Roll Along: Poems on Wheels*
*Why Am I Grown So Cold? Poems of the Unknowable*
(Margaret K. McElderry Books)

**ORIGINAL POETRY**

*Cricket Never Does: A Collection of Haiku and Tanka*
*Flights of Fancy and Other Poems*
*4-Way Stop and Other Poems*
*Higgledy-Piggledy: Verses and Pictures*
*I Never Told and Other Poems*
*Monkey Puzzle and Other Poems*
*Remembering and Other Poems*
*There Was a Place and Other Poems*
*Worlds I Know and Other Poems*
(Margaret K. McElderry Books)

**PICTURE BOOK**

*B Is for Baby: An Alphabet of Verses*
with photographs by Steel Stillman
(Margaret K. McElderry Books)

# I Am
# Writing
# a Poem
# About...

## A Game of Poetry

Edited by

# Myra Cohn Livingston

MARGARET K. McELDERRY BOOKS

**MARGARET K. McELDERRY BOOKS**
25 YEARS • 1972–1997

Margaret K. McElderry Books
An imprint of Simon & Schuster Children's Publishing Division
1230 Avenue of the Americas
New York, New York  10020

Designed by Patti Ratchford
The text of this book is set in Sabon

Printed in the United States of America
First Edition
10 9 8 7 6 5 4 3 2 1
Library of Congress Cataloging-in-Publication Data:
I am writing a poem about . . . a game of poetry :
edited by Myra Cohn Livingston.
p.   cm.
A collection of poems written by members of a poetry master
class taught by Myra Cohn Livingston.
ISBN 0-689-81156-X
1. American poetry—California—Los Angeles.
2. American poetry—20th century.
I. Livingston, Myra Cohn.
PS572.L6I3    1997
811'.548080979494—dc21
97-4098
CIP

Three days after Dad's death, Mom taught her Master Class. Our suggestions to postpone that first session of the term were not well-received. The students were counting on her, and she was not going to disappoint them. With their support, and in their presence, she made her first step into the world as a single person after thirty-eight years of marriage.

Six years later, her strength sapped by illness, Mom rebuffed suggestions that someone take over her class. Whatever energy she had went first to those whose work is represented here. "They need me," she said.

The need, learning, and love were mutual. So this volume is dedicated both to the authors—Mom's second family—and to the lifelong learning that was so important to her, and that is symbolized by their work together.

—*The Children of Myra Cohn Livingston*

# Contents

## Acknowledgments

The Editor and Publisher thank the following for permission to reprint the copyrighted materials listed below. Any existing rights not here acknowledged will, if the publisher is notified, be duly acknowledged in future editions of this book.

Excerpt reprinted with the permission of Scribner, a division of Simon & Schuster, from *My Brother: A. E. Housman* by Laurence Housman. Copyright 1937, 1938 by Laurence Housman; copyrights renewed © 1965, 1966 by Lloyds Bank Limited.

Excerpt reprinted with the permission of the Society of Authors as the literary representative of the Estate of A. E. Housman.

Excerpts from the pre-publication version of UNTITLED POEMS by Alice Schertle to be published by Harcourt Brace & Company. Copyright © 1997 by Alice Schertle. Reprinted by permission of the publisher. All rights reserved.

All poems are used by permission of the authors, who control all rights:
Martha Robinson for "After Rain," "At the Lake," "Morning at Joshua Tree."
April Halprin Wayland for "As I turn my head," "Bongo."

Tony Johnston for "Cloud Tracks," "The Great Drum," "In a Cornfield."

Ann Whitford Paul for "I wonder where wild," "News from Rabbit," "A Ring Needs."

Joan Bransfield Graham for "In the flower bed," "Summer," "Celebration by the Sea," "Duets."

Anita Wintz for "Mused an expert magician named Babbit," "Riddle," "For a Sailor."

Janet S. Wong for "No More," "Oh, Brother!," "After Eighteen."

Alice Schertle for "Three Words Set Sail."

Kristine O'Connell George for "Of Rabbits and Fences," "Rabbit I., Rabbit II.," "Did You See Them?," "The Weaver," "Goddess."

Ruth Lercher Bornstein for "Rabbit," "Lullaby," "Language."

Deborah Chandra for "Rabbit," "To a Dinosaur."

Monica Gunning for "Rabbit."

Madeleine Comora for "Rabbit's Feet," "Grizzly."

Ruth Feder for "When lettuce shoots—*Pop!*—" "Morning," "Sorrowful, Sorrowful."

Karen B. Winnick for "Wild Rabbit," "When Dad Comes Home."

Peggy Leavitt for "A Summer Hum."

Acknowledgments

# Introduction

In his book *My Brother, A. E. Housman,* Laurence
Housman recalls evenings of literary diversions in
the family household. One of the games Laurence
describes is that of the "writing of short poems,
containing a collection of nouns, each member of the
company supplying one." As an example he mentions
"the sort of thing which Alfred was able to turn
out in the course of fifteen or twenty minutes." The
nouns were: *hat, novel, banker, cucumber, yacht,* and
*abridgement.* This is how Alfred handled it:

> At the door of my own little hovel,
> Reading a novel I sat;
> And as I was reading the novel
> A gnat flew away with my hat.
> As fast as a fraudulent banker
> Away with my hat it fled,
> And calmly came to an anchor
> In the midst of the cucumber-bed.
>
> I went and purchased a yacht,
> And traversed the garden-tank,
> And I gave it that insect hot
> When it got to the other bank;
> Of its life I made an abridgement
> By squeezing it somewhat flat,

And I cannot think what that midge meant
By flying away with my hat.

I was reminded of this bit of nonsense recently when
two of my children bought me, for Christmas, a game
consisting of plastic magnetized words which are to be
attached to the refrigerator and (hopefully) turned into
poems. Opening the gift, I immediately remembered a
demonstration I saw many years ago by John Oliver
Simon of the California Poets-in-the-Schools Program
in which he suggested that words written on pieces of
paper be thrown out in the middle of the floor and
used in poems. Similarly I have seen rubber stamps,
each with a word, offered to the young as an
enticement to write. Some educators have suggested
the use of "word bowls" from which slips of paper
are pulled out and given as an incentive for creativity.

There are certainly many schools of thought as to
the use of words in themselves as a stimulus to writing.
Some believe they prod the memory and produce
images, while others feel that inspiration comes not
from single words but from an image or idea; that the
words will follow the initial thrust of what needs to be
said. There is the famous story of Lewis Carroll, the
Reverend Charles Lutwidge Dodgson, who wrote his
poem *The Hunting of the Snark* based on the phrase
"For the Snark was a Boojum, you see," which kept
running through his head one day as he walked in
Oxford. In this instance a particular series of words
sparked a charming bit of nonsense that ran for 639

lines leading up to the use of the phrase.

Thinking about some of these approaches, I became interested in what would happen if I gave words to my master students at UCLA, most of whom are now published poets, and I suggested one day that each write a poem in which the word *rabbit* appears. Once the poems were read at the next class meeting, we were all astounded not only at the various forms chosen, from free verse, quatrains, couplets, and limericks to haiku and cinquains, but by the diversity of voices as well as thoughts.

To continue the assignment for another week, I suggested each person write down a noun and turn it in, and we would choose three words on which to base the second poem. Thus the words would hold more meaning than a commercial game and be controlled by the writers themselves. The words selected—*ring, drum,* and *blanket*—appealed to everyone.

About the last assignment—a six-word-based poem—there was some debate. Everyone was agreed that *hole, friend, candle, ocean, bucket,* and *snake* presented possibilities, but a few preferred the word *scarecrow* to *bucket,* so a choice was given. *Hole, friend, candle, ocean,* and *snake* were mandatory, but one could choose either *bucket* or *scarecrow* as the sixth word. What resulted from this assignment is an amazing group of imaginative poems. In one instance, the word *candle,* which does not appear in the limerick itself, was incorporated into the title!

All of us discovered that the decision to work with

the same nouns not only makes for a keen insight into individual response, but becomes even more fascinating when one considers how images may spring to mind that might never have come but for the juxtaposition of certain nouns, how the imagination is fired by this juxtaposition, how some nouns may turn themselves into other parts of speech, and how some words seem to suggest particular forms for expression. Alice Schertle noted in particular that the discipline of using specific words might well be likened to working within the framework of a small box, yet, paradoxically, it allowed an expansion that led her to move in directions she would not otherwise have taken. Ordinarily, she observed, the idea of associating a scarecrow with the ocean would be ludicrous, but somehow—it not only worked, but worked brilliantly!

These three assignments thus became not only a game, they more than answered the old idea that poets like to "play" with words. Sometimes this play turns into nonsense, as in the case of A. E. Housman and certain of the verses that follow. But oftentimes serious poems result. Whatever the tone, the poets who participated found it absorbing and mind-stretching to get together, decide on a particular group of nouns, and initiate one version of the game. Other possibilities and variations for all those who read this work and wish to play their own games are, obviously, unlimited!

*Myra Cohn Livingston*
*August 1995*

# One Word: *Rabbit*

*After Rain*

Towards evening the clouds that held the rain
parted like two curtains, and the sun
shone in between as if upon a pane
of mirror glass to turn the desert sand,
the rocks and rabbit bush to golden flame.

*Martha Robinson*

I Am Writing a Poem About...

As I turn my head
sideways, a dark rabbit hops
onto the full moon.

*April Halprin Wayland*

*Cloud Tracks*

The sky is full of clouds today,
winter white and light and low.
I'd like to leave my tracks on them
like a rabbit in the snow.

*Tony Johnston*

I wonder where wild
rabbit will live now that the
bulldozer is here.

*Ann Whitford Paul*

In the flower bed
next to the rabbit's ears, a
tulip grows shorter.

*Joan Bransfield Graham*

Mused an expert magician named Babbit,
"If multiplication's a habit,
　　　The worst of my fears
　　　Is an increase in ears
On the nights that I pull out a rabbit."

*Anita Wintz*

*News from Rabbit*

I like to hide inside my den,
down deep beneath the earth,
and listen to the noise Worm makes
squirming through the dirt.

I like to hear Ant in his hill
chewing bits of bread
and Dandelion's feathered seeds
landing overhead.

I love to hear the Snail go gliding
on his slippery trail,
and Lizard every time he flails
his silver-armored tail.

But there's a noise that I like best
to hear beneath the ground
and that's the clump of all your steps—

I love your walking sound.

*Ann Whitford Paul*

I Am Writing a Poem About...

## No More

They promised
we would get a rabbit next.
But hamsters were the last—
frogs, fish, finches, all
our small pets
put in dusty boxes,
buried in the backyard.
Those stupid hamsters,
squeezing through
the bars of their cage
to slip beneath
the living room
into the dark heating duct
where we found them,
stiff, the next day.
Dad blew into his hands,
bringing the golden one
back to life five or ten long seconds,
as long as I held my breath—
no more.

I have eaten rabbit, once,
roasted on a spit in France.

*Janet S. Wong*

*Poem About Rabbit*

I am writing a poem
    about

    rabbit.

A pink-eyed poem
    that watches
            from the
edges
of the page,
    that nibbles
            at the
corners
of my mind.

A quiet poem.

The kind
    with long-eared lines that
listen
    to where the words fall.

A poem
coming close
    enough to touch,
standing

still

to watch
me write a poem
about

rabbit.

*Alice Schertle*

*Of Rabbits and Fences*

Rabbits
appreciate
how this new fence we've built
keeps them safe as they dine on our
garden.

*Kristine O'Connell George*

I Am Writing a Poem About...

*Rabbit*

Your nose
twitches, rabbit;
are your watching your world
move and sprout and rise up in green
again?

Your ears
quiver, rabbit;
do you feel the blooming
of a green song, is it filling
your heart?

Little
wild-born rabbit,
hiding away from me,
you are silent, so I will sing
for you.

       *Ruth Lercher Bornstein*

*Rabbit*

A warm-night-deep-in-June rabbit,
Color-of-the-moon rabbit,

Round-and-shiny-eyes rabbit,
Tippy-toed-and-shy rabbit,

Crouched-where-nothing-stirs rabbit,
Warm-bones-and-damp-fur rabbit,

Hush! . . . The hunters pass.
Shiver in the grass.

Bam! They grab their guns!
Don't look back!
Just run!

Trippety-trip with whiskers stiff
Over field and over furrow
Up a bank and into your burrow.

Hid-and-never-found rabbit,
Made-of-silk-and-down rabbit,

A warm-night-deep-in-June rabbit,
Color-of-the-moon rabbit.

*Deborah Chandra*

*Rabbit*

Tired of its summer hole,
Rabbit, with the nimble feet,
Finds my garden, hops around,
Seeks a tasty meal to eat.

Nibbles carrots to bare stubs,
Whiskers twitch with pure delight,
Hearing footsteps, ears stand straight,
Rabbit flashes out of sight.

*Monica Gunning*

*Rabbit I.*

Coyote?
      Tail flicks.
Dog?
      Quiver.
Fox?
      Whiskers twitch.
Owl?
      Shiver.

*Rabbit II.*

Frightened?

Fearful?

Flight is habit
when life
is wrapped
in fur
of rabbit.

*Kristine O'Connell George*

I Am Writing a Poem About...

*Rabbit's Feet*

Long ago
Rabbit's feet
were delicate
and round,
but Coyote chased him
day and night.
He ran so hard
his feet grew long
and flat.
This slowed him down.
He stopped.
And with those feet
made one great leap
to the moon.

*Madeleine Comora*

When lettuce shoots—*Pop!*—
through spring earth, rabbit,
uninvited, comes to dine.

*Ruth Feder*

*Wild Rabbit*

Twitches at the smell
of fresh-ground coffee.

Sniffles in the dish
of butterscotch toffee.

Scratches at the top
of the dining table.

Burrows in the wood
as much as he's able.

Nibbles at the legs
of the high-back chair.

Nestles in my pocket,
wiggles way down there

to a place soft and deep,
where wild rabbit

snuggles in to sleep.

*Karen B. Winnick*

# Three Words:

*Ring, Drum,*

*Blanket*

*A Ring Needs*

A ring needs a finger,
a blanket, a bed.
A window needs curtains,
and butter needs bread.
A king needs a crown
and so does his queen.
A drum needs a drumstick;
A movie, a screen.
A clock needs two hands.
A door needs a knob.
And how would the corn
grow without any cob?
A cupcake needs frosting.
The shore needs a sea.
These words need a reader.
The reader is me.

*Ann Whitford Paul*

*At the Lake*

A ring around the moon,
Chill in the air—
Too soon to know if
Tomorrow will be fair.

Tonight we spread our blanket
On the cooling sand
Close by the campfire
And hold each other's hands.

We sing the songs of campfire,
But hear the muffled drum
Of camps and summers ending,
Of autumn days to come.

*Martha Robinson*

*Bongo*

With bongo, blanket and Panama hat
I went to a special drum store.
There were drums and drums and drums and
      some
I'd never seen before.

A man was fixing the broken ones
Way back in a small, dark room.
"What's wrong?" he yelled from faraway.
I called, "It doesn't boom."

He came from behind a snare drum rack,
Pulled off bongo's punctured head.
He threw that skin and the tacks away.
"Needs a new head," he said.

"It'll take some time." But I wanted to stay
To witness his drumhealing powers.
He gathered his tools and he turned on a light,
Soaked a new skin in water two hours.

When it was soft, he stretched it tight
To the drum with a metal ring.
"Skin wire," he explained as he squeezed the
      glue.
Then he hammered new tacks 'round the thing

And said, "Come back in a day or two."
So next day I was back at his shop.
He put my drum between his knees
And I watched while his fingers popped.

They pounded! They stuttered! They skated!
        They breezed!
In the middle, along the rim—
I'd never heard my drum do that!
And all because of him.

So I gave my blanket and Panama hat
(As that was all I owned)
As pay to the man who fixed my drum
And I walked my bongo home.

*April Halprin Wayland*

*Did You See Them?*

Did you see them
late last evening,
        fairy lads and lasses
        dancing among grasses?

Here are
        rings of trampled grass,
        acorn drums,
        milkweed lutes
        and honeysuckle flutes.

Here is
        where they slept,
        drowsy from dance,
        nestled and settled
        in blankets of petals.

Did you see them
as the moon was rising?

        *Kristine O'Connell George*

*Grizzly*

A blanket
of lumbering
dried earth
and moss
goes rumbling.
A mountainous back
shakes the trees,
gouges and claws
a century of rings.
The heavy breath
is the dark sound
of winter's
slow drumming.

*Madeleine Comora*

*Lullaby*

Softly, a far-off drum will beat for you,
Clearly, a wind-chime bell will ring for you,
And at night when the stars shine down on
       you,
I will wrap you in a soft cloud blanket
and hold you and rock you and sing to you.

*Ruth Lercher Bornstein*

## Morning

Woodpecker wakes early.
He drums, drums, drums,
making rings in our tree.

I pull the blanket
over my head, and
go back to sleep.

*Ruth Feder*

*Oh, Brother!*

The little squirt,
begging for boiled eggs and toast,
circles me like a wrestler in the ring,
bouncing on my bed,
bouncing,
bouncing,
bouncing,
bouncing,
and when I try to hide my head,
he dives under the blanket,
to drum my stomach
until it surrenders
a growl.

*Janet S. Wong*

*Riddle*

With sticks and with hands
it is beaten in bands;

on top is a skin
like a blanket tucked in;

it's as round as a ring
or the crown of a king.

*Anita Wintz*

(a drum)

## Summer

Ring around
the seasons,
dilly-dally-dum,
feel the summer
coming,
beating on her
drum.
First, it's only
tapping,
then it starts
to boom,
pounding
on the pavements,
marching
in your room.
Throw off
your blankets,
pile them
on the floor,
pull up
the windows,
open up
the door.
No way
to stop her,
dilly-dally-dum,

when hot-blooded
summer
decides to beat
her drum.

*Joan Bransfield Graham*

*The Great Drum*

Someone is beating the great drum
again.
The rumble shakes
the thunderheads.
The sky splits
    with light.

Rain
        rings
                down.

Then
like a Navajo blanket grows
on a loom,
overnight the desert
                blooms.

*Tony Johnston*

## Three Words Set Sail

"Beat the *drum! Ring* the bell!"
I shouted. "This is going well!"
The first two words in record time
were floating on a sea of rhyme,
one sitting forward, one word aft;
my poem was a sturdy craft.
Then one more climbed aboard,
      and  *blanket*
was the word that finally sank it.

*Alice Schertle*

## To a Dinosaur

You hid
like a sun
under the black blanket
of the swampbed,
invisible
but for those bones.
How they flashed—a dead giveaway!
You hide,
we seek,
it's a game we play.

We pull from the earth
the rings of your ribs,
drumbeat of your heart,
the whole vast animal of you.
            Once terrible and feared being.
Hide and seek—it's the game we play.
But time is up.
What?
Our turn, you say?

*Deborah Chandra*

## The Weaver

The warp is tightly strung
like skin across a drum.
The weaver kicks the treadle
which lifts the clacking heddles.

I watch. A picture grows
each time the weaver throws
the shuttle with the weft—
reaches for the catch,
then snaps the beater back.

Painting circles, rings,
the rounded shape of things
with threads stretched straight and taut,
she weaves a blanket, soft.

*Kristine O'Connell George*

## When Dad Comes Home

I love whenever Dad takes trips.
He comes home in a day or so,
his arms all filled with gifts.

On Mom he slips a silver ring,
then wraps me up inside a blanket,
lifts me high and starts to sing.

I bring out drums. We march around,
tell jokes and laugh, whenever Dad
comes back from going out of town.

*Karen B. Winnick*

## Six Words:

*Hole, Friend,*

*Candle,*

*Ocean, Snake,*

*Bucket* or

*Scarecrow*

*After Eighteen*

We finished this round of golf
with our same silly rituals,
me scraping the grass from my spikes
with a lucky half-burnt birthday candle,
my brother sticking the pin into the hole
as if stabbing a snake.
He reached deep into
the bucket of sand and seed,
throwing one scoop of each
to the ocean,
to the desert,
to the mountains,
and then, for the first time,
the scoop he always throws to a friend
he threw to me.

*Janet S. Wong*

I Am Writing a Poem About...

## Celebration by the Sea

My friend
and I scoop out
a hole in the sand, a
bucket to capture our own small
ocean.

We build
a castle cake.
Water snakes through its halls.
Mud turrets rise and on top—one
candle.

*Joan Bransfield Graham*

## A Summer Hum

Gonna walk on my hands,
point my toes,
let the rain
fall up my nose.

Gonna dig a hole,
crawl right in,
serenade a mole
on my violin.

Gonna move a mountain
with my tin bucket.
If it doesn't work,
just gonna chuck it.

Gonna burn in the sun
without suntan lotion.
If I get too hot
gonna jump in the ocean.

Gonna bake a snake
in a special pot pie.
If he wiggles away
gonna sit down and cry.

Gonna cook my crayons
for a rainbow candle.
I'll keep it in a holder
with a twisted handle.

I'm just about finished.
It's just about the end
so I think I'll eat some cookies
with my very best friend

but not until

I walk on my hands,
point my toes,
and let the rain
fall up my nose.

*Peggy Leavitt*

*Duets*

*Candle/Snake*

Wrap two
words around each
other—"candle," "snake"—now
the candle starts to move, the snake's
tongue flames.

*Bucket/Hole*

Of course,
every one
of those shiny buckets
has a big hole—how else would you
fill it?

*Friend/Ocean*

Friend, if
you rub two words
together like sticks, you
may need an ocean to put out
the fire.

*Joan Bransfield Graham*

*For a Sailor*

The lighthouse
is a burning
candle, like
a stalwart
friend who
stands upon
the ocean's
shore, solitary
as a scarecrow
guarding seas
of waving grain.
Its beacon is
a flame that
burns a hole
into the mist,
lighting up
the darkness
of the night;
beaming forth
its silver
snake across
the surface
of the sea—
tossing out
its towline
to rescue me.

*Anita Wintz*

*In a Cornfield*

The night was dark. There was no moon.
A scarecrow stood knee-deep in gloom,
When through the ocean of dry corn
He heard a slight and shuffling sound.

The stuffed man lit a candle then,
And with a rustle, he leaned down.
He saw a snake twist from a hole,
A rippling slip of candle-gleam.

"Good evening, friend." The scarecrow
    smiled.
"We share this withered field, it seems.
How good to know I'm not alone."
But like the moon, the snake was gone.

*Tony Johnston*

*Language*
(for Helen Keller)

This is about a funny word, "scarecrow,"
A slithery word, "snake,"
About the word "water" dropped into a child's
      palm
That grew into an ocean of meaning
And lit a bright candle in her darkness.
It's about a round word, "hole,"
A plain word, "friend":
This is about the miracle of language.
This poem is about understanding.

*Ruth Lercher Bornstein*

*Goddess*

Goddess made Earth
Smooth, round and full.
This was good.

She dreamed hole, and
Scooped out Earth's crust
With her golden bucket.
This was good also.

Goddess dreamed water, and
Filled oceans and rivers.
This was good.

She dreamed light, and
Touched her golden candle
To the sun.
This was warm and good.

Snake slipped from the lake.
(Goddess did not dream this.)
Snake spoke and said,
"What next, Goddess?"

"You," said Goddess.
"You are my first friend."
This was good.
Very, very good.

*Kristine O'Connell George*

*Morning at Joshua Tree*

Rippled, like an inland ocean,
the desert stretches west.
Through cholla* spikes a cactus wren
comes flying from her nest.
Yucca blossoms, giant candles,
on the hillside glow.
A tortoise plods along a path
only he would know
and skillfully avoids the hole
mice might be sleeping in.
Hummingbirds are near. We hear
their chittering begin.
Each claims the clump of yellow flowers
blooming in a niche
in rock that's near the tent my friend
and I and Father pitched
last night. Beyond us Joshua trees
dot the sands and make
scarecrow shapes. Beneath a bush
a snake.

*Martha Robinson*

---

*Pronounced *choy-ya,* a kind of sharp-needled cactus
prevalent in Joshua Tree National Park. The cactus
wren makes her nest deep inside its spiky branches.

## Scarecrow

Last night, alone, he saw the rising moon
set silver fires among his stalks of corn
and watched the tassels burn like candle wicks.
At dawn he saw the noisy crows return.
They know him for a friend, this man of sticks
in boots that dangle just above the dirt,
the handle of a rake shoved through his shirt.

On summer days when grass around him sways
like wave that follows wave upon the ocean,
I've seen him shake, a dancer on a stake,
as if he feels a music in the motion.
And once I saw his round astonished eyes
observe with more than painted-on surprise
a black snake flow like water down a hole,
and heard him sigh upon his wooden pole.

*Alice Schertle*

*Sorrowful, Sorrowful*

Sorrowful, sorrowful, jimjack shop,
Got things for sale but no one will stop.
Got pans full of holes and candles can't light.
Ain't got much else 'cept a broken old kite.

Sorrowful, sorrowful, jimjack store.
Got a snake from the ocean in a bucket on the
     floor.
But if anyone should want him I'd say
     "Certainly not!"
'Cause that snake in the bucket is the only
     friend I've got.

*Ruth Feder*

I Am Writing a Poem About...

# Index of Titles